A Note to Parents

For many children, learning math is difficult and "I hate math!" is their first response — to which many parents silently add "Me, too!" Children often see adults comfortably reading and writing, but they rarely have such models for mathematics. And math fear can be catching!

The easy-to-read stories in this **Hello Math** series were written to give children a positive introduction to mathematics and parents a pleasurable re-acquaintance with a subject that is important to everyone's life. **Hello Math** stories make mathematical ideas accessible, interesting, and fun for children. The activities and suggestions at the end of each book provide parents with a hands-on approach to help children develop mathematical interest and confidence.

Enjoy the mathematics!

• Give your child a chance to retell the story. The more familiar children are with the story, the more they will understand its mathematical concepts.
• Use the colorful illustrations to help children "hear and see" the math at work in the story.
• Treat the math activities as games to be played for fun. Follow your child's lead. Spend time on those activities that engage your child's interest and curiosity.
• Activities, especially ones using physical materials, help make abstract mathematical ideas concrete.

Learning is a messy process and learning about math calls for children to become immersed in lively experiences that help them make sense of mathematical concepts and symbols.

Although learning about numbers is basic to math, other ideas, such as identifying shapes and patterns, measuring, collecting and interpreting data, reasoning logically, and thinking about chance are also important. By reading these stories and having fun with the activities, you will help your child enthusiastically say "**Hello, Math,**" instead of "I hate math."

—Marilyn Burns
National Mathematics Educator
Author of *The I Hate Mathematics! Book*

To Rachel, with love
— Aunt Gracie

For Debbie, Chris, and Chris,
who keep good time
—M.H.

Copyright © 1997 by Scholastic Inc.
The activities on pages 27–32 copyright © 1997 by Marilyn Burns.
All rights reserved. Published by Scholastic Inc.
HELLO READER!, CARTWHEEL BOOKS, and the CARTWHEEL BOOKS logo
are registered trademarks of Scholastic Inc.

Library of Congress Cataloging-in-Publication Data

Maccarone, Grace.
    Monster math school time / by Grace Maccarone; illustrated by Marge Hartelius;
    math activities by Marilyn Burns
        p.   cm.—(Hello math reader. Level 1)
    Summary: From the time they get up at six in the morning until they go to bed at eight o'clock at night, monsters spend a busy day, especially at school. Includes
related activities.
    ISBN 0-590-30859-9
    [1. Time—Fiction. 2. Monsters—Fiction. 3. Stories in rhyme.]
I. Hartelius, Margaret A., ill. II. Burns, Marilyn
    III. Title. IV. Series.
PZ8.3.M127Mo 1997
[E]—dc21

97-5035
CIP
AC

18 17 16 15 14 13 12 11

Printed in the U.S.A.   23
First printing, September 1997

Monster Math
School Time

by Grace Maccarone
Illustrated by Marge Hartelius
Math Activities by Marilyn Burns

Hello Math Reader — Level 1

SCHOLASTIC INC.
Cartwheel ·B·O·O·K·S· ®
New York Toronto London Auckland Sydney

At six o'clock, monsters wake.

At seven o'clock,
they make a mistake.

At eight o'clock,
they go to school.

Then monsters learn
a safety rule.

At nine o'clock,
monsters spell.

At ten o'clock,
they show and tell.

At eleven o'clock,
monsters read.

Then each monster
plants a seed.

At twelve o'clock,
monsters eat.

At one o'clock,
they compete.

At two o'clock,
they subtract.

Then monsters learn
a science fact.

At three o'clock,
monsters go.

At four o'clock,
they catch and throw.

At five o'clock,
they paste and glue.

Then monsters eat
a yummy stew.

At six o'clock,
they take a bath.

At seven o'clock,
they play monster math.

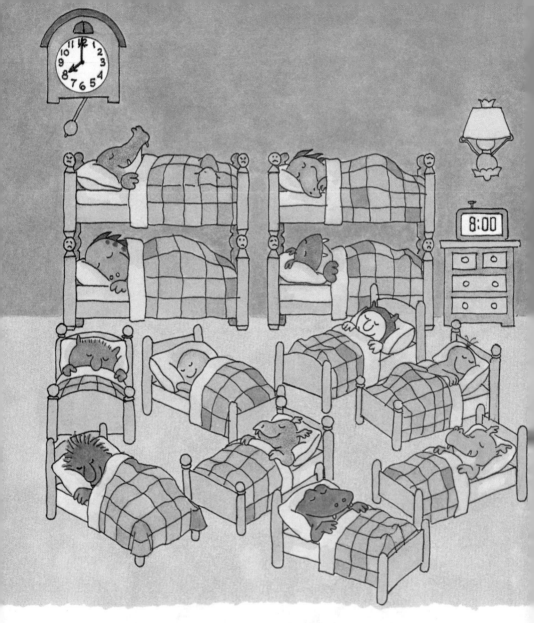

At eight o'clock,
they shut the light.

Monsters are asleep.
Good night!

Children often see people looking at clocks or referring to their watches. "It's 3:30. We need to leave for the movies." "Grandma will be here soon; it's almost 5 o'clock." "You can stay up tonight until 8:30."

Children are familiar with people telling time from clocks and watches, but learning how to tell time by themselves is a complicated process. They need to learn about analog clocks and watches, with two hands or three and with different kinds of numerals. They need to learn about digital clocks and watches. And they need many opportunities for connecting times on all types of timekeepers to their daily routines.

Although it takes some children longer than others to learn to tell time, all children do it eventually. Read the story with your child. If your child seems interested in learning how to tell time, then use the activities to get your child started.

You and your child will also find the Hello Math Reader *Just a Minute* useful and enjoyable for talking about time. The book and activities focus on learning about a specific measure of time — one minute.

— Marilyn Burns

You'll find tips and suggestions for guiding the activities whenever you see a box like this!

Retelling the Story

Read the story again. After you read each page, look at the two clocks in the illustration. Point to each and say what time it shows. (If you need help telling the times, try saying the times along with an adult or an older child.)

What clues on each clock help you tell what time it is?

Now read the story again and try telling the time on the clocks. What are you usually doing at that time?

When the little hand points to the 6 and the big hand points straight up, it's 6 o'clock.

This clock also says 6 o'clock. The 6 is the clue and the 00 tells that it's 6 o'clock exactly!

Note that on four pages, the times are not on the hour. These clocks show 8:15, 11:30, 2:30, and 5:30. Unless your child is particularly motivated, it's not necessary to explain the intricacies of telling these times. Just talk about them as being after 8 o'clock (or 11, 2, or 5 o'clock) but not yet 9 o'clock (or 12, 3, or 6 o'clock).

What Are Your Times?

Try to answer these questions. (You may need help figuring them out.)

What time do you usually wake up in the morning?

When do you eat lunch?

What time is school usually over?

When do you eat supper?

What time does your favorite TV show start? When is it over?

When is your bedtime?

What else do you usually do each day at about the same time? What times do you do these things?

Use routines familiar to your child. If your child doesn't know the times that these routines usually occur, give the information. Then start referring to the clock often during the day whenever your child is doing these activities. While the actual times you do things may not be exact (except for TV programs), the experiences will help focus your child on making sense of what clocks and watches say.

Your Own Time Book

Make your own book of what times you do things on a school day. You can make a book by folding 2, 3, or more sheets of paper in half and fitting one inside the other.

On the front cover, write the title. Use *My Time Book* or anything else you'd like.

For each page, think of a time that you usually do something. Write the time or draw a picture of a clock showing that time. Draw a picture underneath of what you usually do at that time.

If you want to, write a sentence on each page that says:

At _____ o'clock, I _____

_____ .

MY
TIME
BOOK